Do I Really Have to Sleep Now?

Learning the Evening Routine

Inspired by the Montessori Method

"The greatest gifts we can give our children are the roots of responsibility and the wings of independence."

—Dr. Maria Montessori

The Importance of Routines in Montessori

Dr. Montessori's philosophy is rooted in the belief that children need to be as independent as possible; independence helps build a child's confidence, competency, and is also motivating for them. Children also crave order and simplicity, which allows them to focus on the task at hand and eliminates noise.

Routines are incredibly beneficial for little absorbent minds because they are predictable and they allow children to move through them on their own. Through repetition, routines become healthy habits which enable children to slowly build their independence.

Remember to give children your trust, they are more capable than you might think. Where possible, allow your children to operate in a "prepared environment" which fosters confidence and independence. For example, keep their toothbrush and hairbrush in a low drawer they can easily reach or, provide a stepping stool in the bathroom so that your child can reach the sink to complete hygiene related activities.

Our family thrives with routines, so we are sharing some of our own activities on the following pages. We hope you enjoy our suggestions, but also come up with some of your own too – we promise it will be a lot of fun!

The MontiStories Family

To my amazing wife Ana
and super children Alma and Theo
who came into our life
and made it feel complete.

Do I Really Have to Sleep Now?

"Okay, Alma and Theo. It's bath time in about five minutes!" said Alma and Theo's mother.

"Aww, but I don't wanna take a bath!" whined Alma.

Alma and Theo were too busy playing with their train set to even think about taking a bath.

"Look at the clock," said their mother. "It's almost eight o'clock. You know we get ready for bed every night at this time. I'll come back in five minutes."

"Choo choo!" said Theo as he ran the train along the tracks.

"Want to bring the train over here? You are missing a train cart," said Alma smiling.

Theo pushed the train over to where Alma was waiting.

They were very busy playing when their mother came in again. It felt like it had been just seconds ago that she'd talked to them.

"Time to get ready for bed," she said brightly.

Alma crossed her arms in defiance. "Do I really have to take a bath now?" she grumbled.

"Yes," answered her mother. "Do you want to take a bath first or brush your teeth first?"

"Bath..." said Alma grumpily.

Theo and Alma picked up the train set and put it in its box.

Alma grabbed her towel and went to the upstairs bathroom
for her bath. Theo headed to the downstairs bathroom
to brush his teeth.

Soon, Alma was finished with her bath. Doesn't it feel good to
be all clean?" her mother asked.

"I guess so," agreed Alma." Is it time to pick out my book yet?"

"Yes," her mother said, smiling. "But you have to brush your
teeth first."

"Oh! I forgot!" said Alma.

"I'll be right back.
I'm going to go check
on your brother,"
said Alma's mother.

Theo looked through the books in his room for one to read before bed. "Theo, did you have your bath yet?" his mother asked.

"No," said Theo. "But I've brushed my teeth. See?" he said, opening his mouth wide.

"Oh, look at those clean teeth! Well, hurry up. You'll have to have a shower because there's no time for a bath anymore," his mother said.

"Aww, man..." said Theo.

"Both you and your sister are all mixed up about our routine, aren't you?" said Theo's mother.

"There are so many things we gotta do," said Theo.

"I think I have an idea," said Theo's mother, eyes sparkling.

Finally, Theo and Alma were in their pajamas and ready for bed. Each with a book in hand, they waited for their mother to read to them.

But first, their mother wanted to talk about her idea." So, I think we need some practice with our evening routine. Tomorrow, we can make a chart with pictures that shows the different activities we need to complete before bedtime. That way, you can make sure you've done all of them before you pick out your books," said their mother.

"Okay, well, I'm in charge of the pictures," announced Alma.

"I want to help too," said Theo.

"You could do it together?" their mother suggested.

The next day at breakfast, Alma was ready to get started on making the chart. "Can I take pictures of the activities with your phone?" she asked her mother. "Theo can be my model."

"That sounds like fun. Then we can print out the pictures. Let's make a list of the activities we need to include," said their mother. "Do you remember what we need to do before bed?"

"Let's see... We take baths," said Alma.

"And brush our teeth," said Theo.

"We put on our pajamas and brush our hair," said Alma.

"And we read books," said Theo.

Alma and Theo took their dishes to the sink, brushed their teeth, then were finally ready to start working on their evening routine chart.

"Okay, Theo. Get in the tub and pretend you're taking a bath," said Alma, pointing the camera phone at him. Theo grabbed a washcloth and pretended to scrub his arm. "Good! Now pretend you're brushing your teeth," ordered Alma.

"Hey, now it's my turn to take the picture," said Theo.

"Fine," said Alma, handing him the phone and grabbing her toothbrush.

Click! Theo snapped the picture.

"Now it's my turn," said Alma." Put your pajamas on."

Theo hopped into his pajamas and Alma took the picture.

Next, Theo took a picture of a comb and brush. Finally, Alma took a picture of her favorite storybook.

Alma and Theo's mother laughed when she saw all of their great pictures. When they'd printed them all, Theo and Alma carefully cut each one out and pasted them on the poster in order.

"Look! We're all done with our poster!" said Alma, tugging on her mother's arm.

"I see! I can see how carefully you cut out each of the pictures," she commented. "There's just one last thing to do." Their mother gave them a marker and clothespin each. "Write your names on these clothespins."

Alma and Theo wrote down their names. "Now you can clip your clothespin to the activity you're doing so you can keep track," she said.

"Cool!" said Alma and Theo.

"I almost can't wait until bedtime to use it," said Alma. They all laughed.

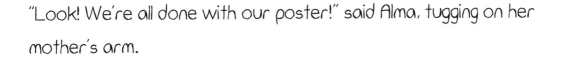

ACTIVITY SUGGESTION:

Make an evening routine chart like the one Alma and Theo made.

Materials:

Poster paper,

scissors,

printer,

glue,

wooden clothespins,

and markers.

＊ If you don't have a printer, you can draw
each activity with coloring pencils instead.

1. Identify the activities in your family's evening routine.

2. Take/draw pictures of each activity in your routine.
   Alternatively, you can also use the *Montessori
   Routines for Children Activity Cards*, part of the
   MontiStories Series.

3. Print and cut out the pictures.

4. Glue the pictures in order on the poster paper.

5. Write your name on the clothespin using the marker.

YOUR POSTER IS READY TO USE!

Other books in the MontiStories Series

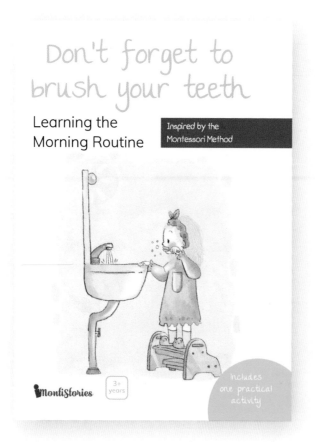

Don't forget to brush your teeth

Learning the Morning Routine

Inspired by the Montessori Method

MontiStories · 3+ years · Includes one practical activity

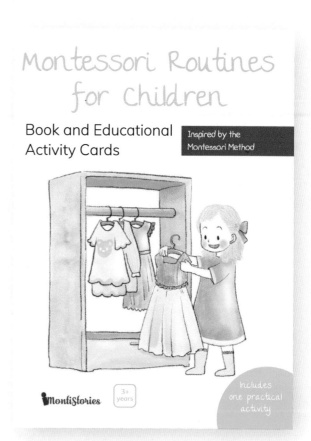

Montessori Routines for Children

Book and Educational Activity Cards

Inspired by the Montessori Method

MontiStories · 3+ years · Includes one practical activity

What are
Germs?

Coronavirus
Update Included

Inspired by the
Montessori Method

MontiStories

3+ years

Includes
one practical
activity

But I'm Scared
to Sleep Alone!

The Importance
of Sleep

Inspired by the
Montessori Method

MontiStories

3+ years

Includes
one practical
activity

Find out more
about Montistories at

www.montistories.com

Printed in Great Britain
by Amazon

25069165R00016